An Amusing Expedition into Life's Quirks

A Collection of Stories from Day-to-Day life

Priyanka Malhotra

INDIA • SINGAPORE • MALAYSIA

Contents

Contents

#1

A Trip to London

Before I recount my adventures in London, let me first express the sheer enchantment that this city holds. As one of the most visited cities globally, London offers a little something for everyone: from its rich history and culture to fine cuisine and unforgettable experiences. The city's vibrant culture welcomes both tourists and residents with open arms.

Allow me to share some of my personal experiences:

- While visiting a popular tourist spot in London, I found myself in need of someone to take my photograph. That's when I noticed two young girls speaking Hindi nearby. I approached them, asking if they were from India. They replied, "We're from Pakistan, but does it really matter?"

I wholeheartedly agreed, saying, "Absolutely, well said. The tensions between our countries exist primarily due to political drama. In a third country, we wouldn't even notice the difference between our nationalities. We share the same language, lifestyle, culture, and bond over food."

The girls acknowledged this truth, took my photo, and went on their way. I genuinely enjoyed our brief interaction and the connection I felt with these two girls from Pakistan. As I returned to my hotel, I reflected on the day's events, and this particular encounter gave me pause. The complex and hostile relationship between India and Pakistan stems from numerous historical and political events. Yet, I couldn't help but wonder – had things unfolded differently, perhaps our countries could have enjoyed a peaceful relationship.

— One aspect of London that I truly admire is the city's commitment to pedestrian crossing. Signalized pedestrian crossings can be found at virtually every corner of the metropolis. These crossings play a vital role in London's walking infrastructure, with the belief that pedestrians should receive equal priority to motor vehicles. Designed to prioritize road traffic, pedestrians patiently wait for the lights to change, allowing them ample time to cross the road—a courtesy not often found in many countries. This approach ensures pedestrians can cross safely without the fear of being struck by a car.

— The London Underground, frequently referred to as the Tube due to the shape of its tunnels, is among the oldest metro systems in the world. For alternative public transportation options, London's extensive bus network provides an excellent choice for shorter journeys. A bus fare in London costs **approximately** £1.65, granting passengers the opportunity to admire the city's landmarks from ground level.

All buses, tubes, and trams feature clearly marked priority seats for those who need them. However, it is common courtesy in London **for younger passengers to offer their seats to elderly individuals or pregnant women. This considerate behaviour is one of the many fine qualities I have observed in London – again not often found in many other countries.**

During my first solo trip to London, I discovered though this city caters to diverse interests, from its rich history and culture to exquisite cuisine; however, **being alone** in such a vibrant city could be **disheartening and isolating at times**.

Despite this, I found that the people of London were incredibly friendly and helpful. Whenever I asked strangers on the street for directions, I encountered only positivity. The city's diverse mix of nationalities, religions, and cultures creates an atmosphere of acceptance and understanding.

It's important to note that London can be an expensive city too, so having sufficient funds is essential in the form of credit cards, cash, and an Oyster Card – a unique transportation card for London. Most establishments in the city accept contactless payments only.

For sightseeing, I relied on Google to find the best places to visit in London. While I could suggest a few attractions, however, everyone has their own preferences, so consulting Google for London sightseeing locations offers a more neutral perspective.

During my trip, I had an amusing experience while trying to visit Wimbledon Court. After taking the tube to the nearest station, I entered a nearby shop to ask for directions. The shopkeeper seemed confused and directed me to a Magistrates' court instead. Smiling, I explained that I was a tourist seeking the famous tennis venue, not a court of law. After repeating "tennis court" a few times, he finally understood and guided me to the correct location.

This light-hearted incident further emphasized the helpful nature of Londoners. In a professional context, I found that colleagues in London offices were equally supportive and dedicated to their work. They remained focused on collaboration without engaging in gossip or holding grudges. With top-notch infrastructure and security arrangements, London offers an excellent environment for both work and exploration.

#2

Corporate Offsite

Once upon a time in the land of corporate wonders, there was an annual event that every employee eagerly anticipated – **the Corporate Offsite**. This magical event was a blend of business and pleasure, a chance for colleagues to bond, learn, and grow together. Little did they know that a whirlwind of hidden agendas would be swirling beneath the surface of their offsite adventures.

Employees embarked on their journey with diverse intentions – some sought relaxation and indulgence, while others reluctantly attended, yearning for exhilarating adventures. A portion of the group seized the offsite opportunity for shopping and sightseeing, whereas others prepared for imminent performances. Amidst the amusement and laughter, even senior management could not restrain themselves from engaging in an occasional strategic gambit.

During one of the days, the organizers had planned a delightful day of shopping and sightseeing. With excitement bubbling, the employees boarded their respective buses, and off they went. Upon arrival, they scattered, each exploring the charming destination.

One employee, let's call her Sarah, found a beautiful red stole that she simply couldn't resist. As she purchased the stole, she realized her hands were already laden with shopping bags. A helpful friend, Rachel, offered to hold the red stole while Sarah adjusted her other bags.

Unbeknownst to Sarah, Rachel had placed the stole in a common area before disappearing into a nearby temple to pray.

As the employees continued their shopping extravaganza, they kept a watchful eye on the time, ensuring they would make it back to the bus by the agreed-upon hour. The offsite had been meticulously planned, with a detailed agenda provided to each employee to avoid confusion and chaos. Time flew by, and soon everyone had to return to the buses, their shopping escapades completed.

As the buses made their way back to the hotel, Sarah inquired about her red stole. To her dismay, Rachel revealed that she had misplaced, and wasn't able to explain any more as the buses were about to leave.

With separate buses to board, Sarah and her friend Rachel found themselves apart, unable to further discuss the whereabouts of the red stole. Upon returning to the hotel, Sarah confronted Rachel once again about the missing item, only to learn that it had been left in the common area while Rachel had visited the temple. Panicked, Sarah and another friend retraced their steps, only to discover that the beautiful red stole was gone. The beautiful red stole was nowhere to be found, as if it had vanished into thin air.

Disheartened, Sarah and her friend returned to the hotel. For a couple of hours, Sarah couldn't shake the feeling of disappointment. But as the evening wore on, she accepted that such mishaps were bound to happen in large groups.

Sarah realized she couldn't fault Rachel entirely, as they both shared responsibility for the incident. She didn't want an apology or reimbursement; she merely wished for a little more thoughtfulness from her friend. A simple act of entrusting the stole to another friend or informing Sarah of its location could have averted the unfortunate outcome.

As the offsite continued, the employees learned to navigate both the excitement and the challenges that came with their grand adventure. With each passing moment, they grew as individuals and as a team, recognizing that life's unexpected twists and turns often provided valuable lessons in empathy, communication, and responsibility.

#3

Offsites

During the days of the legendary Corporate Offsites, colleagues gathered for a magical mix of business and pleasure. The senior management team meticulously planned these adventures, choosing locations, booking flights, hotels, and transfers, and assigning roommates to avoid confusion upon arrival.

In two such offsites, I had agreed with a couple of friends that we would share a room—one in the sandy shores of Goa and the other in the picturesque mountains of Nepal. These events were well-orchestrated, with a detailed agenda that included breakfast, team building activities, sightseeing, shopping, high tea, performances, and finally, a DJ party with a lavish dinner.

After a day full of exciting activities, exhaustion would claim us, and we'd retreat to our assigned rooms for some well-deserved rest. During our Goa offsite, I was so tired that I went to my room to sleep while my roommate wandered the beach with our third friend. A stickler for safety, I always locked the door with a latch. Little did I know that I would doze off so deeply that when my roommate returned, she was left stranded outside our room. Despite her persistent knocking and ringing, I slumbered on. Eventually, I awoke and let her in, and we shared a laugh over the incident.

In Nepal, another amusing door-related mishap occurred. An early morning flight had deprived me of sleep, so once we arrived at the hotel, I headed straight to bed. My roommate, who had a performance that evening, went for rehearsal. As was my habit, I locked the door with a latch and then dozed off. My friend returned after 40–45 minutes, rang the doorbell, called my phone, and even enlisted the help of the duty manager, but the door remained steadfastly closed. Finally, I woke up to the sound and opened the door, much to my friend's relief.

In the end, my friend joked that sharing a room with me could be quite hazardous. She was understandably concerned about my well-being and anxious about getting ready for her performance. All in all, these incidents added a touch of humour to our offsite experiences, and I can't help but wonder if I'm the only one who gets into such situations or if I'm just one of the lucky few.

#4

Corporate Social Responsibility (CSR)

Corporate social responsibility (CSR) is a business approach that aims to positively impact society and the environment by adopting responsible practices. By engaging in CSR activities, companies can contribute to the betterment of various aspects of society and promote a positive brand image.

In our organization, we made it a point to engage in CSR activities annually. One such initiative involved selecting an underprivileged school in Gurgaon that needed maintenance, such as cleaning, painting, and other improvements. These schools were often not well-maintained.

Our team would spend the entire day at the school, starting as early as 8 am and wrapping up around 2 or 3 pm, after lunch. Occasionally, we would invite global visitors from the US and UK, who happened to be in our Gurgaon offices, to participate and experience the event.

We would take photos with our mobile phones, documenting the activities for fun on social media and for a more serious purpose on our internal website within our organization.

Group photos, attendance, meals, and the main tasks of cleaning and painting filled the day.

Behind the scenes, a significant amount of time and effort went into organizing the event. Arranging transportation, catering, and cleaning supplies for 500 people was no easy task. Ensuring safety was also of paramount importance. Although the employees were mature and responsible for their own well-being, the management team also played a role in monitoring and ensuring safety in the official premises.

For employees, participating in these CSR activities was a day of enjoyment, as they could contribute to a good cause while their attendance was marked without having to do any office work.

However, participating in these CSR activities was not without its challenges. Many corporate employees in MNCs have a sedentary lifestyle and are unaccustomed to engaging in physical activities for extended periods. After working for 5–6 hours, most of us would be exhausted, covered in dust, and experiencing leg cramps due to our daily routines.

To ensure that our day-to-day work was not affected, the management team made sure that 25% of employees from each department stayed back in the office. This balance allowed the organization to continue functioning smoothly while also contributing to the community.

We typically scheduled these CSR activities during January or February, as the milder weather was more suitable for outdoor work.

Holding these events during the extreme summer months could cause problems for some employees due to the scorching sun and various medical conditions.

Despite the challenges, participating in these CSR initiatives provided employees with an opportunity to contribute to a good cause, step out of their comfort zones, and engage in activities beyond their usual routines.

#5

Indian Relatives

Indian relatives have long been a fascinating source of entertainment, as they seem to have a keen interest in the lives of their extended family members rather than focusing on their own immediate family. They are always ready to provide endless conversation topics and unsolicited advice, regardless of whether it's needed or wanted.

These relatives often display a knack for meddling in the daily lives of others. In fact, there's no need for CCTV cameras in India—relatives and neighbours are more than sufficient. While they may consider it an intrusion if others offer them suggestions, they feel entitled to interfere in everyone else's life.

It's common for Indian relatives to judge others without reason and engage in gossip about others' lives. Rarely do they approach someone out of genuine concern to offer help or support.

This intrusive behaviour often stems from having an abundance of free time. When people have time on their hands, they tend to pry into matters that don't concern them. However, this behaviour is less likely to be observed among busy individuals.

Every person possesses a great deal of energy that, if channelled productively (ideally into revenue-generating activities), could not only improve their own lives but also contribute to the nation's GDP.

Young students often find themselves disliking their relatives, as they tend to inquire about their grades and compare them to those of other children. This adds unnecessary pressure and fosters an unhealthy competitive environment.

In today's society, relatives often ask questions about one's marital plans, even though they may not have any direct involvement in the process. While they might be genuinely curious or concerned, it's important to remember that you have the right to make your own decisions regarding your marriage and future partner.

In the past, families would play a more significant role in arranging marriages and ensuring the compatibility of the bride and groom. However, times have changed, and people now use matrimonial websites and agencies to find their partners, making the involvement of relatives less relevant.

Despite the shift in the matchmaking process, relatives still enjoy attending lavish wedding ceremonies and participating in the celebrations. It's crucial to remember that while their interest in your life might be genuine, you are ultimately the one responsible for your decisions and happiness. Embrace the changes in today's world and focus on finding the right partner for yourself, while maintaining a respectful relationship with your relatives. Remember that their opinions and questions should not dictate the course of your life.

#6

Interview

When looking for a career change, employers will typically ask you to participate in an interview process to assess your character traits, skills, and work attitude. Interviews allow an employer to determine whether you are a suitable candidate for a vacant position or not.

An interview is essentially a conversation between a potential employer and a candidate. It is a selection process designed to help employers evaluate skills, scrutinize personality and character traits, and assess domain knowledge. During this formal meeting, the employer asks questions to gather information from the candidate. Interviews generally occur during the final phase of the recruitment process and assist companies in selecting the right candidate for a job role.

I'd like to share a personal experience from an interview I had about 4–5 years ago:

I went for a job interview at a company, where I found other candidates waiting in the interview area. I took a seat among them. When it was my turn, I entered a medium-sized hall, where a 73-year-old lady with 50 years of experience was waiting to interview me. There were plenty of chairs, and a few more people were sitting at the back of the hall.

The interviewer held a high position within the company. The interview session began with formal greetings and introductions. While she was introducing herself, I realized she was attempting to show off her achievements to the people sitting behind me, who were enjoying a cup of tea. She boasted about how she had helped the company grow significantly over time.

Then she started asking me questions in rapid succession, without giving me enough time to answer each question properly. She would interrupt me in the middle of my first sentence, cross-questioning every statement I made.

During the interview, her facial expressions and eye contact were focused on the people sitting behind me instead of me, which was quite irritating. However, I remained calm and composed as I needed the job for better exposure and for better money. At times, she would be rude before returning to a more normal tone.

I was already nervous, and her behaviour only made me more anxious. As a result, I stammered during the next few questions, which was noticeable to everyone in the room, including the interviewer.

She seemed more interested in flaunting her skills and achievements in front of others rather than conducting a professional interview. This behaviour could have been more appropriate in a casual one-on-one coffee conversation, but it was entirely unnecessary in an interview setting. The 20–25-minute interview was a terrible experience. I would have been fine with rejection, but the negative attitude and unfriendly environment were uncalled for.

After the interview, I went home feeling disheartened—not because I didn't get the job, but because of the unnecessarily hostile environment created during the interview. I expected professionalism, not friendliness, but she failed to meet even that basic standard. Her arrogance overshadowed her accomplishments and the company's success.

In the evening, I called the coordinator from the same firm who had scheduled the interview. He was a part of the interview process and was courteous and pleasant to talk to. I expressed my disappointment with the interviewer's behaviour, explaining that even if I were offered the job, I wouldn't want to work under her. I felt belittled and demeaned during the interview, which was disheartening.

I acknowledged that as an employer, she had the right to provide feedback to her subordinates, but not at the expense of someone's dignity. Her behaviour not only tarnished her image but also the company's reputation. If she continued to treat clients, guests, and interviewees this way, the company's standing would be at risk.

The coordinator sympathized with me but explained that they couldn't confront her about her behaviour due to her age and gender. They felt obligated to respect her based on these factors.

After the call, I couldn't help but think about how people can reach great heights in terms of position and age yet still lack a sense of professionalism.

#7

Micromanagement

No one appreciates having a boss who excessively scrutinizes the day-to-day work of an employee and constantly checks in. This micromanaging behaviour is not only annoying, but it can also hinder professional growth. But fear not, for there are ways to deal with a controlling boss, as I learned during my first job.

Initially, I was assigned to several managers, but one, in particular, was a notorious micromanager. At first, I thought he was just being cautious since our team was new and our London-based colleagues were still streamlining the process. So, I gave him the benefit of the doubt. However, over time, I realized that his micromanaging was over the top, especially when it came to my work.

My habit of jotting down notes and daily tasks in a diary seemed to catch his attention. One evening, he went through my diary, checking my tasks and their completion status. I was furious, but I decided not to act out of anger and wait for the right time to address the issue.

Another issue with my boss was that he never answered calls after his official working hours. While I understand the importance of personal time, leaders sometimes need to be available for urgent matters. I needed to request an early shift for a doctor's appointment, but despite multiple attempts, he never picked up the phone.

Initially, I had given him the benefit of the doubt, thinking he might be busy or away from his phone. But as the calls went unanswered,

I realized that I couldn't ignore my health and attending the doctor's appointment was more important. I wasn't asking for a vacation to Maldives, just a simple early shift, but my boss seemed unwilling to accommodate me.

Due to the constant changes between morning and afternoon shifts, my health was suffering, and my boss appeared to lack understanding. I decided to text my process owner (PO), who was my boss's superior, explaining the situation and requesting the early shift. Had my boss been more open to communication, I might have shown more flexibility and rescheduled the appointment. However, if the other person refuses to accommodate, I'm not willing to sacrifice my well-being.

After texting my PO, he agreed to speak the next morning and approved my early shift request. During our meeting, I explained the entire situation and expressed my concerns about being forced into afternoon shifts despite an initial agreement that I would work morning shifts.

My main goal was to have someone listen empathetically and **provide a neutral viewpoint**.

Thankfully, my PO understood my concerns and assured me that the issue would be addressed.

#8

Money

Money holds a tremendous amount of influence over our lives, granting us the freedom to pursue our desires, express ourselves, and experience the world. A life with money offers success, choice, security, happiness, and so much more.

However, money can also evoke powerful negative emotions within relationships. Financial insecurity can lead to tension and conflict among family members and friends, sometimes causing bitterness and resentment.

Take a look at the following example:

During my school days, I struggled with my weight, prompting me to join yoga and aerobics classes simultaneously in my residential colony. At times, I faced financial constraints, which led to delays in making my monthly payments to the instructors. Although my instructors allowed me to continue attending the classes due to our friendship, I noticed a distinct change in their attitude towards me. They didn't provide me with the same level of attention as other students, which is crucial for avoiding injuries and maintaining proper posture.

While I understand that these instructors relied on the income, their awareness of my financial situation didn't stop them from demonstrating how money-minded they were. However, when my financial situation improved and I began making timely payments, I experienced a sudden shift in their attitude. Compliments about my weight loss and posture started pouring in, highlighting the impact of money on our relationships.

Another incident – in my early days in the corporate world, I was careful to create a budget for myself, allocating portions of my salary to savings, food, shopping, and other expenses. Being a foodie, I often treated myself to delicious meals and coffee from the food court downstairs. However, this didn't go unnoticed by some of my friends, who pointed out that they couldn't spend as much on a daily basis. I gently reminded them that it was my money and my decision, and that I had a budget in place for my other expenses, which were not visible to them. I emphasized that I was simply enjoying the simple pleasures in life, like good food, and that they should focus on their own lives and their own budgets.

Money has the power to transform relationships. Once money is exchanged between friends or relatives, the bond often becomes more business-like, losing its warmth and intimacy. I've witnessed this first-hand among friends and family members.

Greed can rear its ugly head when family property is at stake, leading to changes in wills, accusations, verbal abuse, and bitterness. Property disputes are all too common, with people turning against each other in pursuit of wealth.

Even small misunderstandings involving money can create rifts. I recall a corporate offsite we took several years ago. When we returned, I had a disagreement with a colleague over the expenses, despite her providing a detailed spreadsheet and receipts. Her response to my questions was **less than friendly**, leading me to decide not to argue with her. Instead, I paid her more than the calculated amount to avoid any further conflict. This experience highlighted the impact of money on relationships and revealed the true nature of those involved.

In summary, money has a powerful influence on relationships, often leading to tension and negative emotions. It's essential to be mindful of how we manage our finances and their effect on our connections with others.

#9

Not All Friendships Are Destined to Last Forever

Some friends enter your life for a season, and when it's time to let them go, it's essential to recognize that not all friendships are destined to last forever. At times, these so-called friends may lie to you, insult you, or divulge your deepest secrets out of revenge. Trust me, these friends are not beneficial for your mental health or overall well-being.

One of the most common reasons great friendships don't endure is the ever-changing nature of our lives. Major life events like marriage, having children, moving, or starting a new job can alter both us and our friends.

Some people maintain lasting relationships that go back to their kindergarten days, while others experience frequently changing friendships. Each individual is unique, and that's perfectly fine.

I've observed that there are two types of people:

Type A and Type B

Type A individuals are always on the move, constantly planning and engaging in activities. They rarely stay home, particularly on weekends, and seem to have numerous friends as they jump from one social scene to another.

There's nothing inherently wrong with them; it's just their nature. They appear to have many friendships or, at least, a strong desire for many friends.

Type B people, on the other hand, are more laid-back and enjoy spending quiet weekends at home, immersed in a good book. They might not answer the phone, especially when their Type A friend calls out of boredom.

With fewer friends, Type B individuals are content. Their downtime at home allows them to enjoy hobbies, crafts, cooking, reading, and other activities that don't require a crowd. They find solace in solitude and seem to have fewer friendships.

Well, there's no need to judge Type A or Type B.

Each one has a purpose in life. Some Type A's may be present for a reason or a season, while some Type B's could be there for a lifetime. By being aware of the personality types you encounter, you can better understand where you fit in and how your friends do or don't fit into your life.

For me, the crucial thing to remember is that people and friendships change. And that's okay. After all, **the only constant in life is 'change'.**

People evolve, experiencing different stages. Some mature, while others don't. Some move on and form new friendships, and sometimes we outgrow our childhood friends. The reasons are as varied as the people we meet throughout our lives.

In our professional lives, we encounter individuals who seem like great friends. However, when we leave that job, the dynamic of the relationship changes. Similarly, when a close friend gets married, our friendship inevitably changes. A young friend may join the military and move away, or another might be involved in a car accident and be left behind in therapy.

That's life.

Social media platforms like Facebook and Twitter can create misconceptions about friendship, leading people to believe that having the most friends or being just a tweet away from lasting connections equates to a healthier social life.

For me, there is a vast array of diverse people in the world, and I relish the opportunity to meet them all. Some become mere names on a holiday card list, many join my social circle, and a select few turn into lifelong friends.

I no longer assess friendships based on their potential for long-lasting connections. Instead, I embrace the fact that I've found someone willing to sit down, share their views, and exchange news with me.

People and friends will come and go. There's an old saying: When God closes a door, He opens a window. The same applies to friendships. When one friend moves on, another will take their place. Just don't get stuck in the hallway waiting for it to happen.

I would like to share a personal example:

Alice had been working at an MNC for two years when she decided to take a break for a few months and re-join the same organization or apply to a new company after some rest. Some of her colleagues advised her against leaving the company, suggesting she take some leave instead of a 6–8-month break. However, Alice felt a more extended break was necessary for her mental well-being. Despite her friends' and colleagues' genuine concern, they continuously pressured her not to leave her job. Ultimately, Alice made her own decision and left.

Five to six months later, she re-joined the same company. During her break, her parents made sarcastic remarks about her decision, even though Alice had planned to return to work or join a new company. Her parents failed to understand this and kept bothering her. Alice had preferred to join a new company, knowing that if her parents could make such comments, so could her old friends and colleagues – but she re-joined her old one as she couldn't get new interview calls. When she returned, her fears were confirmed, and her good friend Martha made sarcastic remarks, which deeply disappointed Alice. Despite maintaining her composure to preserve the friendship, Alice couldn't help feeling hurt by Martha's cold behaviour.

As fate would have it, Alice joined a new company 1.5 years later and was happy in her new position. However, her friendship with Martha began to deteriorate, and they eventually stopped talking. Though they never had a significant conflict, it seemed that things weren't meant to be. Both Alice and Martha moved on with their lives, focusing on their own paths.

Losing friends is an inevitable part of life and is sometimes necessary. The loss of a friend, especially a good friend, teaches you about your boundaries, self-reflection, and the kind of person you want to be. Losing friends can be painful, and losing a good friend may feel like losing a part of yourself. When things don't last forever, it can seem as if everything is falling apart.

#10

Parking Situation in Gurgaon

Once upon a time, in the bustling Indian metropolis of Gurgaon, the roads were choked with cars, and parking spaces were rarer than unicorns. The rapid increase in car ownership outpaced the city's ability to provide sufficient parking spaces in both commercial and residential areas. As a result, frustrated drivers were forced to leave their vehicles parked haphazardly on the streets.

In my own experience, the parking situation has been a constant thorn in my side. I've faced this headache in the past and continue to do so in my current residential area. At my previous residence, a three-storey building comprising one family on each floor, a full-fledged feud erupted between my family and the family on the second floor. The dispute over parking escalated to the point of filing an FIR report, which led to mudslinging and a cascade of accusations.

After that unpleasant experience, we moved to a new area, only to find ourselves grappling with the same problem. We were determined to keep our car within sight, parking it just in front of our gate. Despite installing cameras to monitor our vehicle, tensions rose with our neighbour across the street. One day, in a display of sheer pettiness, he placed two enormous stones in our usual parking spot, ensuring that neither of us could use the space.

It's clear that there's an urgent need for smart parking solutions in our cities. These systems can detect available parking spaces in real-time, optimizing the use of on-street parking and facilities in shopping malls, train stations, corporate campuses, and beyond. However, for now, it seems that the struggle for parking will continue, plaguing urban dwellers like an incurable disease.

#11

People Don't Want You to Succeed

Some individuals simply don't want to see you succeed – this is a common occurrence in any field you work in, be it multinational corporations, government offices, sports, the film industry, or any small or large-scale business you run.

The reasons for this behaviour may vary – hidden resentment, insecurities, jealousy – but there will always be people around you who will try to drag you down, criticize you in front of others, and attempt to thwart your success with hidden agendas.

To share a personal example – one of my colleagues seemed determined to make my life difficult. She would point out my errors in front of others, send unpleasant emails with my manager copied, and lodge complaints with the management team, among other things.

Half of the time, these alleged mistakes were not even genuine errors; she simply wanted to assert her point that the management team had no valid reason to re-hire me within the same department. In reality, she was anticipating a promotion in the current quarter, and when I re-joined the team at a higher position, her aspirations of a promotion were dashed. The situation was further exacerbated when I went to London within three months of re-joining the team. This London visit seemed to add fuel to the fire, something she apparently couldn't stomach.

From that point on, her campaign of pointing out my supposed mistakes and filing complaints began.

Her major strength was that she was proficient in her work, possessed intelligence, and had strong managerial skills. However, all of this was overshadowed when she focused her energy on bringing me down.

In addition to involving the management team, she would also badmouth me to clients during the regular weekly calls we had. She had one-on-one calls with them, but I would eventually get wind of her actions, realizing that these incidents were also taking place.

Although I would get angry, I chose to remain silent and never react. My intention was to let her become the villain in others' eyes if she was the one causing a scene. People would judge her character rather than mine. She then tried to be more cunning by complaining to my manager, hoping she would provide me with feedback while she could laugh from behind the scenes. But her efforts were futile. While her actions did upset me, I never responded or reacted publicly, maintaining absolute composure and giving the impression that her behaviour didn't affect me.

For the next two quarters, she didn't receive a promotion. I'm sure this must have hurt her deeply, but even she didn't react.

By this time, she had also calmed down and stopped nitpicking. Meanwhile, I had become more accustomed to the system, familiarized myself with the people, and learned the old and new rules and regulations. If I had been an average performer before, I was now a strong performer with very few mistakes, which effectively halted her complaints to the management team.

Although the cold war between us persisted throughout our tenure, she eventually began engaging in informal interactions with me in the cafeteria, formal meetings in conference rooms, and even organizing fun parties and inviting me to these gatherings.

She never confronted me about what was truly bothering her that led her to start this behaviour, but I knew that not getting the promotion at the right time had deeply hurt her.

However, in the third quarter, she did receive her promotion, and perhaps her anger had subsided by then. But you know how it usually goes – when you don't achieve the desired results on time and face a delay of two quarters, you're bound to feel disappointed. With no expectations left, you adopt a **"we'll see when it happens"** mindset. The excitement fades, and it becomes more of a formality.

So, from her perspective, she wasn't entirely in the wrong, but her actions and reactions were misguided. Ideally, the business wouldn't operate this way, and a win-win situation could have been created for both of us by the management team. However, this is how organizations and businesses often function, leading to conflicts between employees within the same team.

That being said, there are certain scenarios in which some people simply DON'T WANT YOU TO SUCCEED.

#12

Phone Incident

During my first job at Company X, camera phones were not allowed on the premises. This was because some employees would spend time on social media, causing distractions from work. Furthermore, companies in the financial sector often have confidential data that needs to be protected, which was the primary reason camera phones were not permitted in the workplace.

As a result, employees would purchase two phones: a smartphone and a non-camera phone. We were allowed to bring the non-camera phone into the work area for work-related or emergency calls from family members. The smartphones were kept in lockers outside the work area.

One particularly light workday, I went to check my locker and discovered that my smartphone was missing. I searched everywhere and asked my colleagues if they knew anything, but to no avail. It seemed impossible for a phone to go missing from a locked locker.

I approached the HR and Facilities managers to determine the next steps in finding my missing phone. They were genuinely concerned and asked me several questions about the situation. At the same time, I had forgotten about a few scheduled meetings with onshore colleagues in London. Thankfully, these were team calls, and my teammates were able to cover for me. If it had been a solo call, I would have attended, as professionalism is crucial in the workplace.

The HR and Facilities managers suggested that I send them an official email requesting that they review the CCTV footage to look for any clues. They thoroughly examined the footage from the locker area, but unfortunately, no concrete evidence was found regarding the whereabouts of my missing smartphone.

Meanwhile, my friends and colleagues joined the search for my missing phone, believing that there must be a clue we had overlooked. Although I occasionally returned to my desk to work, ensuring my job didn't suffer, I also continued to search for my phone.

My black Apple phone had a Roger Federer back cover, which was the only distinguishing feature to help identify it among the many other black phones.

After 3–4 hours, I finally found my phone. But how?

It turned out that the locker keys provided to employees could open any lock. Another employee had mistakenly opened my locker, thinking it was his because he also had a black Apple phone. He didn't notice **Federer back cover** and took my phone, placing it in his locker. In his excitement, he didn't even check his own phone for what he came for. He wanted to place few calls, but something triggered and he went back.

When he later opened his own locker, which was shared with friends and contained multiple phones, he didn't recognize his own phone and simply left my phone there, thinking it was his. By chance, I spoke with him about the situation, and he opened his locker, revealing my long-lost treasure – my phone.

Although I eventually found my phone, those 3–4 hours spent without it made me realize that losing a phone isn't the end of the world. We often place too much importance on materialistic items and status, but it's not worth it. The real concerns when losing a phone are the loss of contacts, pictures, and other data, as well as the NEW expense and effort of buying a new phone ALTOGETHER.

Before this incident, I never bothered to create a backup for my phone. However, after this experience, I began to regularly back up my phone, which was an important lesson learned.

#13

Promotions

In the fast-paced, modern world, several traits are essential for securing a promotion in a multinational corporation. These include competence, diligence, intelligence, loyalty, and strong social skills, communication, and networking abilities. However, above all, what truly matters is the innate drive to produce the best work possible. Investing in relationships, both internally and externally, is crucial for professional growth.

Experience also plays a key role in promotions, as illustrated by the story below of two employees, Samira and Kaira.

Both at the same level and eagerly awaiting their respective promotions, they found themselves in different positions when promotion announcements were made. Samira was promoted, while Kaira, despite being hardworking and deserving, was not.

Kaira's expectations had been raised by the praise she received from her colleagues, and she had hoped for a promotion in the upcoming quarter. While she harbored no ill feelings towards Samira, her disappointment stemmed from her own unfulfilled expectations. To make matters worse, a third friend unintentionally upset Kaira further by asking if she was okay, which led to her excusing herself to the washroom.

The reason for the difference in promotions was tenureship, as Samira had joined the company before Kaira. Upon learning about the situation, Kaira's manager and HR manager discussed it with the Senior Vice President (SVP), who initially hesitated, believing that Kaira should have better control over her emotions. However, the HR manager explained that Kaira's reaction was typical for someone new to the corporate world, comparing it to college students' reactions to exam results. They assured the SVP that as Kaira progressed in her career, she would gain more experience and better understand the ups and downs of the corporate landscape.

In the following quarter, Kaira was promoted as well. Although she was happy about her advancement, it felt more like a consolation for the previous quarter rather than a genuine reward. It is often said that the joy of accomplishment is greater when it comes at the right time.

Perhaps it would have been better if Kaira's colleagues hadn't raised her expectations, sparing her the disappointment. Nevertheless, this is the reality of the corporate world.

In another scenario, a manager named Venessa was promoted after significantly increasing her visibility and working hard for six months. However, before and after this period, she returned to her routine work and did not continue her extraordinary efforts. This situation raises questions about the motivations and practices behind promotions.

It has been suggested that some individuals may engage in ***inappropriate relationships*** to advance their careers, but this is not the case for everyone.

Moreover, if a relationship between a supervisor and an employee turns sour, it can create a tense work environment, affecting not only the individuals involved but also their colleagues. Thus, it is essential to recognize and celebrate genuine hard work and merit when considering promotions, ensuring a fair and healthy workplace.

#14

Relationships in the Workplace

Navigating romantic relationships in the workplace can be a complex and challenging experience. Some people find success and even lifelong partners, while others may face heartache or even the need to change jobs as a result.

Throughout my work experience, I've witnessed numerous romantic relationships, some of which were successful and others that weren't. However, one common issue is the lack of privacy in the workplace. No matter the type of relationship - be it boyfriend/ girlfriend, husband/wife, or even siblings or in-laws - maintaining a sense of private space can be difficult. Sometimes, one partner may act bossy or dominating, which can be even more challenging if the boss scolds you in front of your partner. While some couples manage to be highly professional and maintain a respectful demeanour, it's still essential to maintain a balance between work and personal life.

In the realm of romantic relationships, there are various types of people and situations:

- Some girlfriends may try to help their boyfriends by getting them a job in the same organization, hoping to boost their careers or provide a kickstart.

- Others might be smooth talkers, wooing their partners with charming words only to leave them heartbroken in the end.

- Some individuals may have a singular goal – to sleep with their partner and then move on, unfortunately ensnaring unsuspecting individuals in their trap.

During annual corporate offsites, some official couples may cling to each other 24/7, neglecting the primary purpose of these events - **cross-functional team bonding.** While it's natural to want to have fun and spend time together, it's essential to remember that corporate offsites are official events with certain boundaries that should be respected, whether ethically or unethically.

If you want to take your romantic relationship to the next level, consider doing so during a personal vacation rather than in a professional setting.

Workplace romances are unique in that they represent a blend of professional and personal lives. In corporate offsites, for example, one incident involved a group of girls who were planning a dance performance. When one participant didn't show up for practice, her husband revealed that she was drunk and unable to attend. While honesty is generally a good quality, but it can sometimes lead to compromising situations or even damage someone's image among their colleagues.

In some organizations, couples may **not** be allowed to have the same hierarchy, which can create opportunities for politics and manipulation by managers.

In other cases, spouses working in the same organization may become suspicious of each other's relationships with colleagues, leading to accusations of affairs or jealousy.

There is also a phenomenon called **"friends with benefits",** where two individuals in an organization may engage in intimate activities without any commitment to each other. These relationships can exist in many workplaces and may blur the lines between friendship and romance.

Regardless of the type of relationship, love stories can emerge at any stage in life and sometimes with unexpected people. In the workplace, love stories often begin when:

- Two colleagues share their daily work experiences with each other, providing a supportive environment for communication.

- Colleagues share meals or snacks, creating a sense of togetherness and sparking a connection.

- A desire to spend more time together grows, indicating a deepening connection between the two individuals.

- Previously mundane tasks or experiences, like coming to work or making eye contact, become exciting and enjoyable.

These small gestures can ignite the spark that leads to love stories in the workplace. While navigating office romances can be complicated, they can also be a source of companionship, support, and, ultimately, love for those involved.

#15

School Days

Certainly, I'm not here to impart wisdom about the nostalgic school days; rather, I wish to share my experiences from both school and the corporate world.

School undoubtedly serves as the foundation for our education, fostering lifelong friendships and creating cherished memories. While it may seem that we were free from financial concerns back then, but we undoubtedly faced significant stress from homework, exams, and strict teachers - a sentiment shared by many students.

As I listen to contemporary stories from children and their parents, I can't help but feel that the pressure has significantly increased compared to our time. Although I'm not entirely certain, it seems that the course syllabus has expanded to some extent, contributing to the heightened stress.

I'd like to share a few experiences that have left both positive and negative impressions, along with some unconventional lessons:

Bookmarks - I first discovered bookmarks during my school days. To be honest, I had no idea what a bookmark was or its purpose until my history teacher introduced me to the concept. Rather than using a traditional bookmark, she advised us to use a colourful ribbon with a piece of cello tape attached, marking the page where she should begin checking our notebooks, instead of having to flip through multiple pages.

Mail Products - I first learned about various mail products, such as letters, inland letter cards, postcards, parcels, telegrams, and book packets, through a school skit. While our syllabus only covered letters, this program introduced me to the other mail products, which I still remember to this day.

In today's fast-paced and modern age, emails and the internet have largely replaced traditional letters. Although letters still exist, I assume they are used to a lesser extent, as emails offer a quicker and more economical means of sending messages, which can include text, images, or animations.

Pen friend – This concept, also part of our syllabus, referred to a person with whom one becomes friendly by exchanging letters, typically through postal mail. Also known as pen pals, these individuals are often strangers whose relationship is primarily based on letter exchanges, and sometimes even entirely so.

Lunch Time – Lunchtime used to be the highlight of the day. Not because of the food, but because it provided a much-needed break from monotonous lectures and an opportunity to hang out with close friends. It's amusing to think about the critical decisions we made each day about where to sit during lunchtime.

Exam Time – Let's face it, everyone cheats during exams. One of my friends would always bring chits (tiny notes) and coordinate with the top students to ensure they passed with flying colours. Cheating nowadays also involves earphones, which can be helpful but risky if caught. This method requires wearing long sleeves or jackets, having long hair to hide the wires, and using earphones with buttons to play the next audio.

During our 10th standard board exams, our Maths teacher, knowing there were a few average students who might struggle to pass, unofficially told us that if we found a golden opportunity, we were free to cheat.

From picnics to annual functions – While many of my peers may have fond memories of participating in annual functions, my experience was somewhat different. I recall classmates being involved in multiple performances, rushing from the stage to the green room to change costumes. But whenever I volunteered to take part in an act or help with administrative tasks behind the scenes, I was often met with discouragement. Teachers would say, **"By looking at your face, we can't think that you'll be able to do it."** This happened several times, which was quite disheartening, especially coming from a teacher.

Of course, this doesn't mean I never participated in any annual functions, sports day events, or picnics. My main point is that discouraging a student is not the solution. **Judging someone's abilities based solely on their appearance is unfair.**

Moving on to the next class was always thrilling, as was the scent of new books, notebooks, and stationery.

Pin-drop silence during history or geography lessons, or when the vice principal entered the classroom, was another memorable aspect of school life. As soon as they left, we would make a lot of noise.

Our history and geography teacher was incredibly strict, often compared to Hitler. While her subject knowledge and teaching methods were excellent, her strictness was excessive. Most teachers were amazing and helpful, but some were overly dominant. Looking back, I realize that politics were present not only in the corporate world but also among teachers and students.

While some may disagree with my perspective on teachers, I am sharing my personal experience. I have encountered many exceptional teachers and maintained good relationships with them. However, a few bad apples can change the entire atmosphere. Unnecessary insults, sarcastic remarks, and making students' lives miserable were, unfortunately, part of our day-to-day experience.

In conclusion, despite some negative experiences, the memories of school life remain a treasure to cherish. When reminiscing, it's never about grades or tests; it's about the memorable moments shared with our best friends.

#16

School Fetes

School fetes are among the most eagerly awaited events of the academic year. They offer students a much-needed break from their routine and a chance to celebrate and have fun. Additionally, school fetes provide an opportunity for the school to raise funds for various projects and improvements. Students also benefit from taking on responsibilities during the event, which helps them develop skills beyond academics. While most schools host annual fetes, some opt for smaller events held more frequently to give students regular breaks from their daily grind.

I recall a particular school fete from when I was in the 11th grade. The date was set, and responsibilities were assigned to all the students. My house was conveniently located just across from the school, only a two-minute walk away.

On the day of the fete, I attended primarily to avoid being marked absent. After spending some time at the event, I returned home for lunch. Unfortunately, a misunderstanding led to an argument between my mother and me, and she scolded me for some reason. I don't remember the specifics of the disagreement, but it left me feeling a bit upset. Nonetheless, I continued to have my lunch.

During events like School Fetes, Annual Day Functions, or Sports Day Functions, some students take advantage of the situation to sneak out and meet their friends or significant others. One such incident involved a schoolmate of mine, whom I'll call Sushmita.

For school fetes, not only are teachers and students invited, but families and friends from outside the school are also encouraged to attend, in order to maximize participation and engagement. Sushmita had informed her family about the upcoming fete and invited them to attend, although she was quite certain they wouldn't show up.

On the day of the fete, Sushmita arrived at school, marked her attendance, and spent an additional 10–15 minutes there. When she saw an opportunity, she slipped out of the school, unaware that someone from her family might actually attend the event.

In those days, mobile phones were not yet common, so Sushmita couldn't be easily reached. To her surprise, her mother and younger sister arrived at the school to attend the fete. After searching for Sushmita for a good 15–20 minutes, her mother came to my house. To this day, I'm not sure how she knew where I lived. It's possible she asked another student at the fete about Sushmita's friends, and they mentioned my name and pointed out my nearby house.

So, Sushmita's mother rang my doorbell while I was having lunch. I got up to answer the door and met her mother and sister for the first time. After exchanging greetings, Sushmita's mother explained that she couldn't find her daughter at the school premises. Although I didn't know where Sushmita was either, I started to suspect where she might be. Her mother seemed to know what was going on and where her daughter could be, but she wasn't worried about kidnapping. I could read her face and guess what she was thinking.

To assure her that I genuinely didn't know anything and to clear my own name, I accompanied Sushmita's mother and sister back to the school to search for her, especially since my parents had started to suspect me as well, and I had already had a fight with my mother earlier.

We searched for Sushmita for a good 10–15 minutes before I excused myself, telling her mother that I didn't know anything and had come only because she insisted. She thanked me, and I returned home. It was evident, though, that she was quite upset and angry with her daughter.

The following Monday at school, I asked Sushmita what had happened and where she had been. She told me that she had seized the opportunity to meet her boyfriend, not realizing her mother would attend the fete and ruin her plan. When Sushmita got home, her mother was ready for a thorough interrogation, scolding, and punishment.

I felt sorry for Sushmita, but there was nothing that could be done. She eventually broke up with her boyfriend. To keep a closer eye on her, Sushmita's mother began picking her up and dropping her off at the bus stop where the school bus arrived, among other surveillance measures.

#17

Stolen Items

Once upon a time, in a bustling metropolis, there was a multinational company that had offices scattered across the world. Their employees worked diligently to connect businesses from all corners of the globe. Every now and then, international visitors would travel to their Indian office to discuss important matters, and it was the job of me and my team to ensure their stay was comfortable and hassle-free.

One sunny day, a prestigious guest from the UK visited the office. As always, my team and I took care of his every need, from hotel accommodations to car transfers. After a series of productive meetings, the visitor bid adieu and boarded his flight back to the UK.

The dedicated team managed the visitors' agendas, ensuring that lunches, dinners, meeting rooms, car transfers, and hotel arrangements were all taken care of. Sightseeing was a rare occurrence, as the guests were primarily there for business matters.

During one particular visit, an esteemed guest inadvertently left his innerwear in his hotel room before boarding a flight back to the UK. The hotel staff, having somehow obtained my number, contacted me to inform me of the situation. At first, I found the incident both surprising and amusing. However, I quickly realized that it was simply a lapse in human judgment, not an intentional act. My amusement turned to concern as I now faced the responsibility of returning the forgotten items to the guest in London.

I requested the hotel staff to send the guest's belongings to my office. Though initially reluctant, they agreed to deliver the items, considering the short distance between the hotel and the office.

Upon receiving the parcel, I securely stored it in a locked drawer at the office, opting not to take it home in case of a burglary. As fate would have it, a break-in occurred at the office as well, which operated in three shifts: the Indian shift from 8 am to 5 pm, the UK shift from 1 pm to 10 pm, and the US shift from 4:30 pm to 1:30 am. I worked the UK shift, from 1 pm to 10 pm.

On the day the parcel arrived, I locked it in my drawer and went home. As part of my routine, I checked the drawer every day to ensure the parcel remained safe and untouched. Then, one day, I checked the drawer as usual, but found only one packet remaining. In reality, there were two packets. The burglar had stolen one, leaving the other untouched, containing only socks and miscellaneous items. I was shocked and immediately informed my manager.

We conducted an investigation, questioning everyone on the team to find out if anyone had seen someone forcibly open my drawer and take out the item. I even checked with the US shift team, but they had no knowledge of the incident. They, too, were baffled as to who would steal used innerwear.

My suspicions turned to the office cleaning team, who cleaned the desks and chairs after the night shift. I obtained the necessary permissions to access the CCTV footage to investigate the incident further. However, after reviewing the entire footage, I found no concrete evidence. I was left feeling disheartened and unsure of what to do next.

I knew that another visitor from the same London office was scheduled to arrive in two months. I had initially planned to hand over both packets to this visitor, who would then return them to their rightful owner upon her return to London. Now, however, I could only give her one packet.

I discussed the situation with my manager once more, and he suggested escalating the matter to senior management, including the

SVP and VP, in search of a resolution. My manager and I approached their office and explained the entire scenario. They questioned us relentlessly, as though we were the culprits. Nonetheless, I understood that they were simply conducting a thorough inquiry to find the best possible solution.

The SVP responded with a remark, "Oh my goodness, this is so embarrassing," before delegating the matter to the VP. My manager and I followed the VP to his office, where he said to me, "Priyanka, you should have taken this home instead of keeping it at the office." I replied, "Sir, burglary can happen anywhere, even at my home. There's no guarantee it wouldn't have happened there. If a home is considered safe, then so should the office be, where CCTV cameras are installed to catch anyone attempting theft."

His suggestion made me feel that if the items had been stolen from my home, the senior management might have easily blamed me and taken extreme action against me. I asked if

I could explain the entire scenario in an email to him, but he taught me a crucial lesson: **"Never ever document anything like this in an email. It becomes a written record and can be used against you."** Instead, he advised me to call the guest and relay the entire situation. I agreed and scheduled a call with the guest for the next day.

During the call, I explained the entire incident to the guest, who listened patiently. In the end, he reassured me, "Relax, Priyanka, these things happen. Never mind. Besides, I've forgotten what was in the packet, and I didn't even know I left anything behind at the hotel. It's okay."

#18

The Young Detectives

During my childhood, there were three of us who were good friends. Let's call them Joan, Vicki, and Harriet. The names are hypothetical. Joan and Vicki had been close friends since early childhood, and I (Harriet) joined their friendship later. The two of them shared a strong bond, and I got along with them quite well.

As teenagers, Joan and Vicki were strikingly beautiful and had lovely facial features, which made it easy for them to attract boyfriends or crushes.

In the evenings, we used to go for walks together. A group of boys would often join us on these walks. Among them was a boy who took a liking to Vicki, and over time, he proposed to her. Let's call him X.

Vicki and X started developing feelings for each other and began talking on the phone regularly. X would share various details about his life, such as living in the same neighbourhood or owning a particular car. Initially, Vicki believed what he said and didn't suspect anything.

One day, during our usual evening walk, Vicki noticed X walking with another girl in the park. X didn't realize that Vicki had seen him with this girl, and Vicki felt a bit upset, wanting to find out who the girl was.

The next day, when X called Vicki, she couldn't contain her curiosity and asked him about the girl he had been within the park. Since X hadn't noticed Vicki seeing him in the park, he lied and said the girl was his sister. This made Vicki even more suspicious, sensing that something wasn't quite right.

The three girls, Joan, Vicki, and Harriet, decided to investigate the matter further, becoming a trio of little detectives. They planned to go for a walk the next morning instead of their usual evening stroll.

The young detectives went to the address X had given to Vicki. They rang the doorbell, and a girl answered, informing them that no one by the name of X lived there. It was a three-story building, and X didn't live on any of the floors. This was their first piece of evidence.

Next, Vicki looked up the phone number X had given her, which they used for their daily conversations. Back then, telephone directories were widely used. She cross-referenced the name with the number, considering the possibility that the number might be registered under his father's, grandfather's, or an uncle's name with the same surname. However, the directory listed a completely different surname.

They also ruled out the possibility that it was a friend's number, as X had told Vicki it was his private number for her to call without hesitation. This was their second piece of evidence.

X had mentioned owning a car but sometimes came to meet Vicki on a motorcycle. Vicki, being sharp, noted the motorcycle's registration number without X realizing. She recalled the number, and they suggested she contact one of her school friends whose family had connections at the RTO office.

Vicki did just that, and within a few days, she learned that the motorcycle had been stolen. This was their third piece of evidence.

Vicki decided to break up with X, giving a random reason for the split. She didn't want to let him know that they had gone to the extent of checking his home address, phone number, and vehicle registration number. They couldn't be sure of his real intentions, and revealing his true identity to him could potentially cause unforeseen problems.

#19

Visitors

As hosts, we often have to cater to a variety of visitors in both our personal and professional lives. Professional visits are typically planned in advance, as international visitors need to book flights and hotels well ahead of time. In India, we are known for our exceptional hospitality. We take care of numerous administrative tasks for our guests, including creating agendas, scheduling meetings, arranging transportation, organizing meals, booking meeting rooms, handling IT requirements, and much more. A lot of work happens behind the scenes to ensure a smooth visit, with everything carefully planned down to the serving of tea and coffee.

However, an unfortunate incident occurred in the past. One of our esteemed visitors, let's call him George, was planning to visit India for a week after being away for a year.

George was a mediator between our process and our clients. His primary role was to secure business, address escalations, respond to queries or problems that a specific team might have, and work to resolve them.

As George's visit date was quickly approaching, preparations were in full swing at the Indian office. He was coming from the USA.

However, just one day before his visit, we received news of his sudden death due to a medical condition. Everyone was shocked. We all had plans to speak with him, not only professionally but on a personal level, and share our experiences. But it seemed that fate had different plans for him. It was a truly shocking incident for all of us.

In another instance involving a visitor named Richard, he developed a crush on one of our team leaders and proposed to her. Such romantic gestures are not entirely uncommon.

Regarding the duties I mentioned earlier, where we had to arrange numerous things for our visitors, one visitor, named Hazel, commented to the team after their visit, "Please be organized next time." This comment was made despite the extensive effort and planning that had gone into making the visit a success. Such feedback can be disheartening for teams that work tirelessly to ensure a successful visit.

Last year, an incident occurred where approximately 7–8 visitors were scheduled to visit our office simultaneously, and naturally, everything needed to be arranged from scratch. My immediate supervisor, Keshav, assigned another colleague, Geeta, to assist me in managing the preparations. Three years ago, when the coronavirus pandemic and lockdown began, a work-from-home model was introduced. However, last year, around

June/July, the number of cases had decreased, and people had started venturing out as the government eased certain restrictions. In response, our office implemented a hybrid model, combining work-from-home (WFH) and work-from-office (WFO). When numerous visitors were present, employees were required to come to the office for the entire duration of the visitors' stay, whether it was one week, two weeks, or more.

Although Geeta occasionally offered helpful support, she was mostly **intrusive**. As she was senior to me in both age and experience, I restrained my thoughts and hesitated to express my concerns to her. My primary focus was to ensure that our work did not suffer, so I allowed her to do as she pleased. Despite finding her behaviour irritating, I kept my feelings to myself since she was also assisting me.

One day, we were at the office, and it was already 6:30 pm. My meetings for the day were over, and I was planning to go home. Generally, I tend to work late into the night—until

11 pm, midnight, or even 1 am—to complete any pending tasks, regardless of whether I went to the office that day. Whenever I return home from the office, I freshen up a bit and then resume work. Geeta noticed me and suggested that I complete a particular task before leaving. I explained that I was going home and would continue working on my laptop to finish the task before the day's end. I understood the importance of the task and its timely completion, but I requested to do it after returning home. If the task had been urgent, I would have completed it on the spot. Geeta then inquired about my mode of transportation home, to which I replied that I travel independently and call a personal taxi.

Afterward, Geeta made a few phone calls and checked one of our internal websites before informing me, "Priyanka, you're entitled to company transportation. Why don't you use it?"

I responded, "Because I feel **uncomfortable**. While I understand that using company transportation might be safer, I don't want to waste my time in a cab with 10 other colleagues from different zones, waiting for everyone to be dropped off one by one, which would take around 1.5 hours. Taking a personal taxi would get me home in 25–30 minutes. If I feel uncomfortable, that's how I feel. Besides, how does using a personal taxi instead of an official one affect my productivity? I'm spending my own money from my salary, yet it still seems to bother you."

At that moment, my immediate supervisor approached and told me, "Priyanka, don't worry, I'll drop you off. My house is in the next sector, so your home is quite close by."

I couldn't refuse his offer for obvious reasons (as he being the boss). I was already planning to work until 11 pm or midnight **voluntarily at home**, but due to Geeta's intervention, I ended up working in the **office** until 11:30 pm. I didn't mind working late, but her approach was entirely wrong.

The story didn't end there, though. The next day, she repeated her suggestion, asking me why I didn't use the company's official cab service and again the same conversation continued.

Some people will never change.

#20

X'mas Gifts

The festive season was around. The office looked lively with, twinkling lights and the scent of gingerbread cookies filled the air. It was time for the annual Christmas party, a much-anticipated event that celebrated the hard work and dedication of the company's spirited employees throughout the year. In previous years, they'd paint the town red at a swanky venue, but this time they decided to bring the merry cheer right to the heart of their workplace.

In the spirit of camaraderie and togetherness, the employees were instructed to buy gifts for each other, within a specified budget, to place beneath the office Christmas tree. With 10–11 teams, comprising 400–500 members, the gift exchange was carefully orchestrated to ensure nobody received their own gift.

In one corner of the office, a subtle cold war brewed between Suzie, an ex-boss, and Samantha, a team member under her supervision. Samantha's husband, X, was also a part of the company, and he was well-aware of the tiff between the two women. X was given the responsibility of distributing the gifts, alongside Santa, during the festive event.

As the employees excitedly lined up to receive their presents, X spotted Suzie approaching. In a moment of mischief, he discreetly swapped the large gift he was holding for a smaller one, handing it to Suzie with a wry smile. The Senior Vice President (SVP), who was overseeing the event, noticed the exchange but chose to remain silent to keep the party atmosphere alive.

After the event, the SVP approached Suzie at her desk, inquiring about the gift she had received. As fate would have it, Suzie had been given a **Laughing Buddha - a symbol of happiness, contentment, and prosperity.** Suzie couldn't help but appreciate the irony, even as she acknowledged the unprofessional behaviour displayed by X.

Although the SVP likely addressed the issue privately with X, the incident served as a valuable reminder to all: professionalism isn't just about appearances, but also about how we conduct ourselves with responsibility, integrity, and accountability. It's about communicating effectively, appropriately, and always finding ways to be productive.

And so, the employees of the company learned a vital lesson that Christmas season: professionalism should always triumph, even in the face of personal disagreements. For when we put aside our differences and focus on our collective goals, we can achieve greater success together.

#21

Make-Up

In today's world, makeup has become an integral part of many people's daily routines. Individuals use makeup for various reasons, with the most common one being to accentuate their natural beauty. Numerous makeup and cosmetic products are available, such as lipsticks, powders, concealers, and body shimmers. Another interesting aspect of contemporary makeup is its ever-changing nature, influenced by social media trends and celebrity fashion.

In our current lifestyles, makeup has become indispensable. While it's essential to feel comfortable in one's natural appearance, makeup can provide an extra boost to self-confidence. Celebrities often rely on makeup to maintain their youthful and vibrant looks, both day and night. Several ingenious makeup inventions have transformed the art and fashion industries.

Makeup Brushes

The right brushes can significantly enhance makeup application, benefiting everyone from highly skilled makeup artists to those who prefer minimal makeup.

It's worth investing in a few essential brushes, such as high-quality blush, eye shadow, eyebrow, and eyeliner brushes. Fortunately, finding good brushes isn't difficult.

To determine which brushes you need and which ones are of high quality, familiarize yourself with various styles, shapes, and bristle types.

Before buying brushes, it's essential to know what you're looking for and which brushes are worth the investment. Evaluate a brush's quality by testing how the bristles feel against your skin and running your fingers through them to ensure they don't shed. It's also crucial to test how a brush feels when you hold it in your hand.

SKINCARE FUNDAMENTALS

Few individuals possess naturally flawless skin. However, with knowledge, experience, a balanced diet, and exercise, it's possible to significantly improve your skin's appearance. The skin's condition can change daily and vary with the seasons. Factors such as hormonal fluctuations, stress, pregnancy, medication, travel, and seasonal changes can all affect the skin. By recognizing various skin conditions, you can choose the appropriate cleansing methods and moisturizers.

FACIAL CLEANSING & TONING

Cleansers

Cleansing aims to eliminate bacteria, makeup, and the dirt, sweat, and oil that accumulate on the skin each day. It's necessary to clean the skin at least once a day with a formula that doesn't strip it of its natural oils.

Toners

Toners invigorate circulation in the skin, eliminate residual dead skin cells or oiliness, and provide a smooth texture. They can be beneficial for individuals with very oily skin or those who wear a significant amount of makeup. Use a toner after cleansing the skin or as a supplementary cleaner to remove dirt and oil. Toners are particularly useful during the summer when the skin becomes oilier and tends to attract more dirt and bacteria. They also help to maintain the skin's natural pH balance.

Makeup Removal & Skin Cleansing

- Secure hair away from the face using a headband or elastic.

- When wearing makeup, a multi-step cleansing process is often necessary. Begin with a makeup remover or tissue-off cream to dissolve most of the makeup, avoiding the eye area.

- The skin surrounding the eyes is extremely delicate and can be easily irritated. Specific makeup removers are formulated for this area. Dampen a cotton pad with the product and gently rest or press it around the closed eye. Wipe gently.

- Apply cleanser to the entire face. Using a cleanser suitable for your skin type, massage the product into your skin with an upward circular motion. Include the neck, beneath the earlobes, and the chin.

- Rinse the entire face, including the eye area, with warm—not hot—water.

- Dry the face using the softest natural-fiber towel you can find. Gently pat the face dry. Rubbing or vigorous wiping can create small abrasions on the skin surface, causing irritation, redness, and even swelling.

Moisturizers & Sun Protection

Hydration

The most crucial step in skincare is maintaining hydration. The tone and elasticity of the skin depend on the water present in the underlying tissues, which is drawn from atmospheric humidity and moisture applied to the skin's surface. Oil serves as the skin's natural protectant, preventing moisture loss. Oil in the skin acts as a defensive barrier, smoothing the texture and promoting skin cell health. When oil glands overproduce, the skin appears greasy, and when they underproduce, the skin becomes dehydrated and flaky. Providing moisture to the skin helps maintain its firmness, smoothness, softness, and radiance.

Facial Moisturizers

Moisturizers are the true source of youth.

Moisturizers create a barrier between the skin and the environment, retaining water in the epidermis. They hydrate and plump the skin, making it appear smooth and bright. The right moisturizer enhances the appearance, feel, and health of the skin and can even temporarily reduce fine lines and wrinkles. Moisturizers also protect the skin from pollution, debris, and weather. Proper skincare products help makeup apply smoothly, adhere well to the skin, and last longer.

Moisturizing Tips

- Apply a fast-absorbing eye cream beneath concealer for smooth, non-crepey skin. The skin around the eyes is more delicate than the rest of the face.

- For under-eye puffiness and wrinkles, try using a richer formula containing shea butter or beeswax at night.

- If your skin is very dry and dehydrated, use a super-rich moisturizing balm with ingredients like petrolatum, glycerin, or shea butter for improved texture and smoother foundation application. Warm the balm in your palms before applying it to your face.

- Layer different textures of moisturizers for optimal results. For example, combine absorbent creams with balms or oils.

- If you have oily skin, try an oil-control lotion on the forehead and nose to reduce shine. Oil-free formulas hydrate while helping to control overactive oil glands. Foundation applied over the lotion will hold better as well.

- For dry, chapped, or cracked lips, apply a lip balm specifically formulated for lips.

- Create your own sheer, tinted moisturizer by mixing face lotion with foundation.

Sun Protection

Lines, dark spots, and uneven skin texture are often not the inevitable effects of

aging but can result from excessive sun exposure. Overexposure to sunlight can also cause cancer. The skin's worst enemy is too much sun. The only way to prevent premature aging and skin damage from overexposure is to avoid the midday sun when possible, wear protective clothing and hats, and ALWAYS USE THE PROPER SUNSCREEN.

UVA RAYS have the longest wavelength and maintain high intensity throughout the day. They penetrate the epidermis and deep into the dermis, damaging newer cells. UVA rays are hazardous and can cause cancers and sensitivity reactions.

UVB RAYS have a midrange wavelength, and like UVA rays, penetrate the epidermis and reach the dermis. These rays break down the organization of skin cells, leading to wrinkles and broken blood vessels. They are most intense from 10 a.m. to 2 p.m. and near the equator. Glass protects skin from UVB rays.

UVC RAYS have the shortest wavelength and are typically absorbed by the ozone layer. They are absorbed by the epidermis and can be extremely dangerous in large amounts. As the ozone layer thins, attention must be given to these UVC rays.

Tips for Protecting Your Skin from the Damaging Effects of the Sun

- Avoid long periods of sun exposure whenever possible, especially between 10 a.m. and 2 p.m., when rays are strongest.

- Protect exposed skin year-round. Use sunscreen with an SPF of 15 to 30, depending on the season and exposure duration. Long-sleeved shirts and wide-brimmed hats offer some protection. Since the sun penetrates loosely woven and wet clothing easily, wear sunscreen even when covered.

- Wear wraparound sunglasses with 100% UV-blocking lenses, as most sunscreens are too harsh for the sensitive area around the eyes.

- Choose a sunscreen that guards against both UVA and UVB rays, often labeled as broad-spectrum sunscreen. Many popular sunscreens may not adequately protect your skin from these harmful rays.

- Apply liberally—about one teaspoon of sunscreen to your face and at least one ounce (approximately a shot glass) to your body each day. The face and hands are high-risk areas for cancer, so apply generously to those areas.

- Waterproof and water-resistant sunscreens are suitable for swimming or sports. Waterproof products work for ninety minutes, while water-resistant sunscreens last thirty minutes. Apply or reapply twenty minutes before entering the water to allow the product to bond with the skin.

- Those who work outdoors might need frequent application of high-SPF sunscreen.

- UVA rays reflect from all light surfaces, including water, sand, snow, ice, and even concrete.

- Children under six months old should not wear sunscreen but should instead be covered and kept out of the sun.

CONCEALERS & CORRECTORS

Correctors brighten the darkest under-eye areas, allowing concealers to lighten and blend seamlessly. Concealers should blend into your skin, minimizing dark circles and instantly improving your appearance.

Concealers can cover tattoos, spots, blemishes, scars, redness, and bruises, but most people use them to lighten dark circles under the eyes. Different concealers and correctors are formulated for each specific use. Choose a concealer and, if necessary, a corrector designed for each problem area.

Under-eye concealers are not meant for covering blemishes or areas of redness. They have a creamier consistency and are lighter than the skin tone. Using under-eye concealer on redness will only emphasize the imperfections. Yellow-toned foundation that matches the skin tone is the best way to cover blemishes, scars, and tattoos. Proper application of under-eye concealer is crucial in any makeup routine. When chosen and applied correctly, concealer can instantly lift and brighten the face. Select a colour one to two shades lighter than your foundation. The thin skin under the eye reveals the blue hue of the fine veins beneath the surface. A light yellow-toned concealer masks this blue discoloration and brightens the skin. Sometimes a stick foundation one or two shades lighter than the face can serve as an under-eye concealer for those needing minimal coverage.

Correctors are available for extreme under-eye darkness. When a regular concealer cannot fully lighten the under-eye area, a peach or pink corrector is used to counter the purple or green tone. A regular yellow-toned concealer is typically lightly layered over the corrector to brighten the under-eye area. Occasionally, those with extremely deep purple or green coloration under the eye will not require the layer of regular concealer.

FOUNDATION

Beauty starts with great skin. The right foundation will give the appearance of not wearing any foundation at all, leaving you with even-toned, flawless-looking skin.

The purpose of wearing foundation is to even out skin tone and texture. When applied correctly, the result is clear, smooth skin. Most importantly, the skin should look better than it did without foundation.

BRONZER & SELF-TANNER

Bronzers and self-tanners create the appearance of a healthy sun-kissed glow. They can also be used as correctors to warm up the complexion. Applying bronzer adds a healthy radiance all over the face and evens out color differences, especially through the neck. Bronzers work on all skin tones except porcelain, as bronzer can make porcelain skin appear dirty. Self-tanners can be used on the face and body to add color and conceal flaws. Apply self-tanner to the face several hours before applying makeup, and don't forget your neck and ears (remember to wash your palms with soap and water). Bronzer can act as a blush for very dark skin. On all other skin tones, apply blush over bronzer to add a touch of vibrant color.

BLUSH

Blush creates a healthy, attractive look and can also be used for dramatic contouring, as seen in fashion shows and theatre productions. Choose a formula suitable for your skin type and one that you find easy to use. Different formulas can be used depending on the desired finish or time of year. For a natural appearance, match the blush colour to your cheeks when flushed from exercise. You can also pinch your cheeks and match that colour. Comparing several shades of blush next to your cheek will help you identify which ones provide a flattering lift and eliminate those that appear too dull or orange.

The right shade will add a subtle, beautiful brightness to your face without being obvious.

EYES

The goal of eye makeup, whether it's simple black mascara or dramatic contouring shadow, is to make your eyes stand out. Properly applied eye makeup can create the illusion of brighter, more captivating eyes. In this section, we'll cover the basics, such as selecting flattering shades and lining the eyes, as well as advanced techniques like creating a smoky eye and applying false lashes.

EYEBROW SHAPE & DEFINITION

Just as a great frame enhances a painting, eyebrows frame your eyes. Beautifully groomed eyebrows make a significant difference. You can transform a face with just tweezers, shadow, a brow brush, and brow gel. A professional can help you discover your ideal shape, and once your brows are groomed, maintaining them is easy.

All brows can benefit from added definition. Brow brushes and combs quickly tame and shape the brow hair. Brow shapers define, control, and shape the brows effortlessly while adding a touch of colour.

Eyeliner

Eyeliner is the ultimate way to define and enhance the eyes, framing them, making them appear larger, and truly standing out. Liner can also be used to improve the eye shape. It should be applied generously enough to be visible when the eyes are open for maximum impact. Many women achieve a beautiful, defined look using liner only on the top lash line. For those who apply liner on both top and bottom lash lines, it is essential to keep the top line thicker than the bottom to avoid a tired or dark appearance under the eye. Apply a relatively thin or smudged line as close as possible to the lower lash line.

Eye Makeup Removers

Eye makeup removers come in liquid, lotion, and cream formulations. Choose a product that effectively removes your eye makeup without causing irritation or stinging. Generally, non-oily products remove makeup quickly and easily. However, oil-based removers are most effective for waterproof makeup. Place a nickel-sized amount of the product on a cotton ball, and gently press through the eye area to dissolve the makeup. Repeat this process, if necessary, until the cotton ball comes away clean.

Tips:

- Makeup should be simple. With proper application techniques and an organized makeup drawer, it should take only five to ten minutes. Practice is key.

- Pre-Makeup: Moisturizer is essential for fresh-looking skin and creates an ideal base for makeup. Use a lightweight moisturizing lotion for normal skin, a rich hydrating cream for dry skin, and an oil-free formula for oily skin.

- Begin with a lightweight eye cream to ensure that under-eye concealer applies smoothly and evenly.

- Foundation: To find the perfect foundation shade, test a few shades on the side of your face and forehead, and check the colors in natural light. The shade that disappears is the right one.

- Apply foundation with a brush, sponge, or fingers where the skin needs to be evened out, such as around the nose and mouth where redness often occurs. For full, all-over coverage, use a brush, sponge, or fingers to apply and blend foundation to the outer edge of the face.

- To cover blemishes, apply a foundation stick or blemish cover stick in a shade that exactly matches the skin tone. Pat with your finger to blend and repeat if necessary.

Blush

- Smile and apply a natural shade of blush on the apples of your cheeks. Blend upward toward the hairline, then downward to soften the color.

- For long-lasting results, layer a brighter blush on top.

- For an extra glow, dust shimmer powder on the cheekbones with a face blender brush, or use a creamy formula applied with your fingers.

BRIDAL MAKEUP

Bridal makeup should be extraordinary. On her wedding day, every bride should appear as her most beautiful self. It's not the time to try a very trendy or radically different look from her usual style. Wedding makeup needs to be long-lasting, photograph beautifully, and remain timeless. Every bride should love how she looks in her pictures even ten years later.

Makeup Guidelines

- Natural light is ideal for makeup application. If possible, set up your makeup station near a window or use a very bright lamp.

- Use a moisturizer that prepares the skin for makeup. Avoid sunblocks and sunscreens that can cause a "flash off" effect. They reflect too much light under flash photography, resulting in overexposed shots.

- Accentuate the eyes by brightening any under-eye darkness with corrector and concealer.

- Flash photography emphasizes pink tones, so be sure to even out the skin with a yellow-toned foundation. Begin around the nose and mouth where redness occurs, and then blend out to the rest of the face.

- Blend thoroughly, especially at the corners of the eyes, as cameras can pick up visible makeup lines.

- Set concealer and foundation with a sheer loose powder. Applying powder with a powder puff ensures excellent wearability and reduces unwanted shine—essential for picture-perfect results.

MAKEUP FOR TEENS

Many young women are fascinated with makeup but often lack the knowledge, skills, or confidence to make it work. The teen years are a time to experiment with trendy colors and textures, but a youthful face should never be buried under makeup.

- Skip applying foundation all over the face. Cover blemishes with a blemish stick, and apply a stick foundation to areas needing color correction.

- Don't use makeup to look older. The results can appear harsh and awkward.

- Opt for light and sheer colors. Avoid heavy, smoky eye shadow and overly bold shades for lips and cheeks.

- If the skin is oily, keep blotting papers on hand for touch-ups throughout the day.

- To avoid drawing attention to braces, skip bright lip colors. Instead, use a moisturizing tinted lip balm or sheer gloss.

- Use a clear brow gel to keep brows in place.

Career Paths for Makeup Artists

Makeup artists have numerous career options, ranging from long-term positions in television with regular pay and benefits, to freelance work on short-term runway, print, or film projects in various locations and styles.

Department Store Counter

Artists typically work for a specific makeup line, helping customers choose and apply their own makeup. This job involves sales, and compensation is often commission-based.

Bridal

Working with brides is always rewarding. Makeup artists need to conduct consultations and run-throughs, as well as apply makeup on the wedding day. The job often requires traveling to the bride's location and may include makeup application for the entire bridal party.

Beauty Salon

Makeup artists in salons often take on a teaching role. They perform makeovers, help clients practice techniques, and are frequently called upon for special events and weddings. Fashion and media work may also be booked through salons.

Television

Working on a set entails creating character looks, which can range from basic makeup to designing elaborate characters, aging actors, creating the appearance of illness, replicating injuries, and more. Artists may work for years on a single television show. Careers often begin with assistant positions in the industry, and artists develop portfolios and resumes. After gaining experience, artists can join a union, which offers opportunities, job security, medical benefits, and a pension. Most television shows require makeup artists to be union members.

Film & Fashion Show

Filming can take days or months, sometimes in multiple locations. Breaking into the film industry is challenging but not impossible. Large-budget films typically require makeup artists to be union members.

Fashion shows provide numerous media-related opportunities to enhance your portfolio. These events often feature photographers and videographers capturing every aspect of the show, both on the runway and behind the scenes. Many will interview the lead makeup artist to learn about the inspiration and mood of the show. The makeup artist's role is increasingly important in conveying the overall image and look of the fashion show. It's not enough to make the model simply beautiful;

the makeup artist should be able to discuss the designer's vision, current trends, and styles, as well as the inspiration behind the season and collection.

DAILY
Skin Care Routine
1. CLEANSING
2. TONING
Special Skin Caring for Weekends
3. MOISTURIZING
MASKING

Fluffy Powder Brush
Makeup Brushes
NATURAL BRISTLES
Best with powder products
Contour/Blush Brush
Bronzer Brush
SYNTHETIC BRISTLES
Best with liquid or cream products
Highlight Brush

MICELLAR CLEANSERS
Ideal for:
Dry and Sensitive Skin
Face Cleansers
GEL CLEANSERS
Ideal for:
Oily and Combination Skin
CLAY CLEANSERS
Ideal for:
Oily and Combination Skin
OIL CLEANSERS
Ideal for:
Most Skin Types
CREAM CLEANSERS
Ideal for:
Dry and Sensitive Skin
FOAM CLEANSERS
Ideal for:
Oily and Combination Skin

Face Toners
WHAT
Water-based liquids composed of specific active ingredients
WHY
To complete the cleansing of your skin
HOW
After cleansing, saturating two cotton pads, use toner on your face
DIY
GREEN-TEA TONER:
make one cup of green tea, add half a teaspoon of honey. Mix well. After the mixture's cooled, add three drops of jasmine essential oil & pour into an airtight bottle.

Types of Moisturizers
WATER AND OIL EMULSION
CREAM-BASED
FOR
Dry-Skin
GEL-BASED
FOR
Oily Skin
WATER, ALCOHOL, OR LIQUID FAT BASE
LOTION-BASED
Light Moisturizers
BOTH FACE AND BODY

Sunscreen

SUNSCREEN
Summer or winter, monsoon or spring, the need for shielding your skin from the harsh rays of the sun is essential
Sunscreen should be worn daily, no matter your location — indoors and outdoors.
For everyday wear, sunscreen should be applied to the face, as well as other areas of concern.
Always use a sunscreen with SPF (Sun Protection Factor) 30 or higher.
You should reapply every couple of hours.

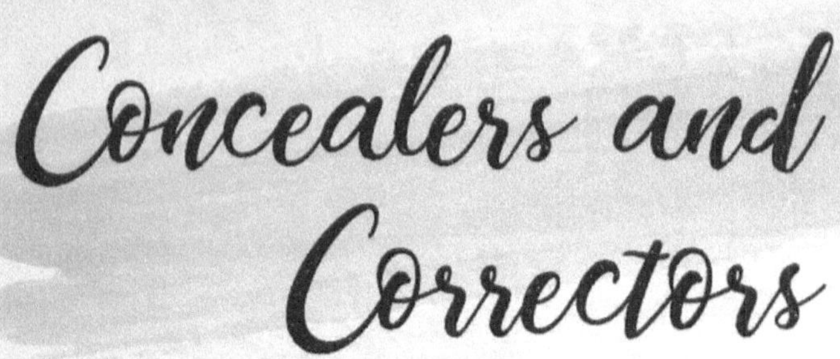

ZITS/ ACNE
EYE BAGS
DARKNESS/ BLEMISHES

Foundation

FINDING THE PERFECT SHADE

✓ Once you have decided on the right formula.

✓ Make sure the foundation is yellow-based.

✓ Test several shades on the side of your face.

✓ Double-check the selected color on forehead

✓ Always test foundation in natural light.

Blush

FIND THE RIGHT FORMULA

For normal to dry skin:
Try a cream blush

For normal to oily skin:
Go with a powder formula

For oily skin:
A gel stays put

CHOOSE YOUR TOOLS WISELY

For bright powder blush, a good fan brush is a must.

A fan or a big, fluffy brush works with other powder blushes.

For cream or gel blush, the best tool is your fingers

FLATTER YOUR FACE SHAPE

Oval faces: Sweep over your cheekbones

Heart shaped faces: Apply to the outer corner of your cheekbone

Round faces: Sweep from the ear down the cheekbone towards the mouth

Long faces: Apply on cheekbones below the outer corners of the eyes

LAYER IF NECESSARY, DON'T OVERFLUSH

Eye Primer
A BASE FOR THE EYELIDS, ABSORBING EXCESS OIL AND ALLOWING FOR AN EVEN SURFACE ON WHICH TO WORK
Make shadows and eyeliner go on smoother and last longer
Help enhance your makeup hues and make them even brighter

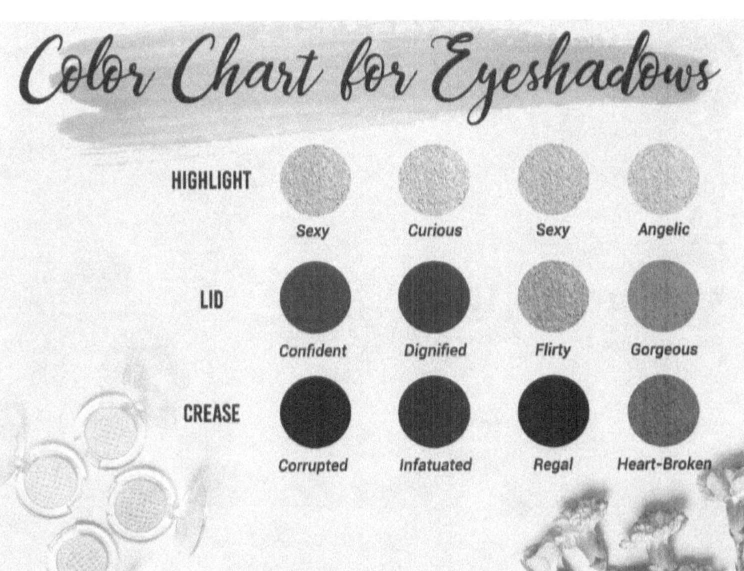
Color Chart for Eyeshadows
HIGHLIGHT
Sexy
Curious
Sexy
Angelic
LID
Confident
Dignified
Flirty
Gorgeous
CREASE
Corrupted
Infatuated
Regal
Heart-Broken

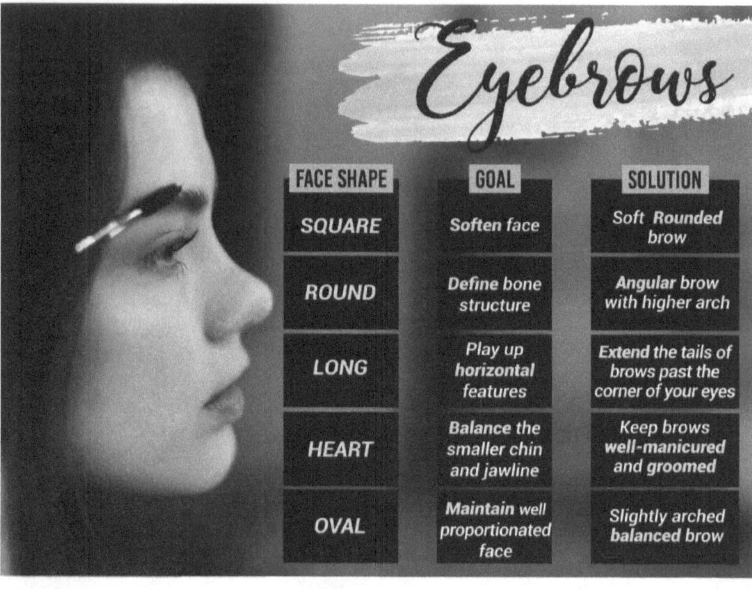

FACE SHAPE	GOAL	SOLUTION
SQUARE	Soften face	Soft Rounded brow
ROUND	Define bone structure	Angular brow with higher arch
LONG	Play up horizontal features	Extend the tails of brows past the corner of your eyes
HEART	Balance the smaller chin and jawline	Keep brows well-manicured and groomed
OVAL	Maintain well proportionated face	Slightly arched balanced brow

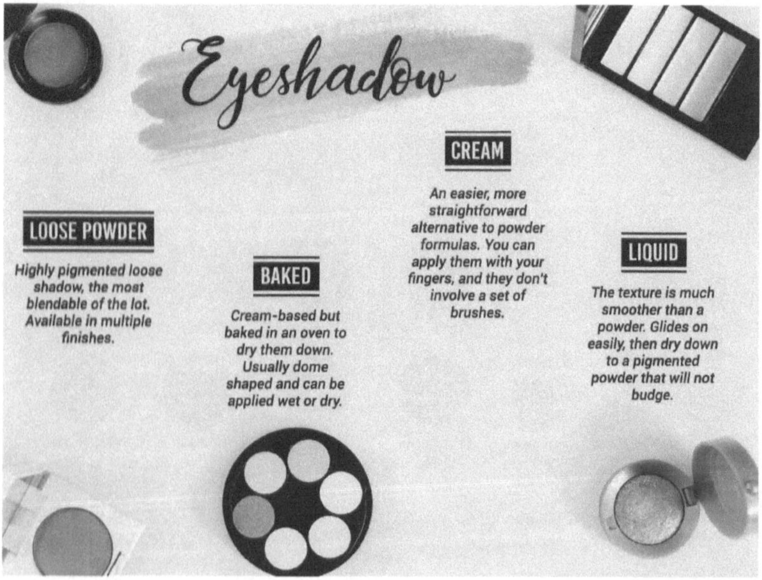

Eyeshadow

LOOSE POWDER

Highly pigmented loose shadow, the most blendable of the lot. Available in multiple finishes.

BAKED

Cream-based but baked in an oven to dry them down. Usually dome shaped and can be applied wet or dry.

CREAM

An easier, more straightforward alternative to powder formulas. You can apply them with your fingers, and they don't involve a set of brushes.

LIQUID

The texture is much smoother than a powder. Glides on easily, then dry down to a pigmented powder that will not budge.

Eyeliner

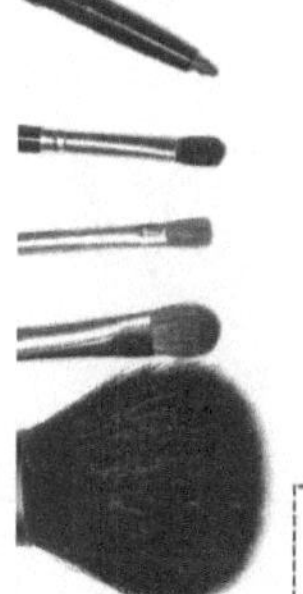

LIQUID EYELINER
(BRUSH TIP)

is great for creating clean lines that swoop or flick. It's for looks that require delicacy and preciseness.

GEL EYELINER

Has a very waxy consistency and is generally applied with an eyeliner brush or a q-tip.

FELT-TIP LIQUID LINER

Allows you more control of the line you are making. A felt-tip doesn't let you add too much product.

KAJAL EYELINER

It's not creamy. Unlike other pencil eyeliners this one won't smudge nearly as easily, even in the waterline.

KOHL EYELINER

intensely dark, smooth, and supereasy to blend. Super easy to apply to the waterline.

Eyelashes

CURLING: *Use supple waxes to soften the lashes, and shape them to have a curved dimension*

LENGTHENING: *Contain fibers are particularly good at extending lashes. Are applied with hard rubber applicators with very short, dense bristles*

VOLUMIZING: *Often contain silicone and/or minerals — which plump and nourish the lashes — and tend to dry faster, allowing you to build multi-layer volume more quickly.*

THICKENING: *Has rubbery bristles spaced really far apart, as far as mascaras go. As you comb it through your lashes, the mascara thickens each lash from root to tip, while the bristles keep them separated and unclumpy.*

Day Look

Bridal Makeup

PICK A WARM CHEEK COLOR

Cream blushes in warm peaches or pinks give skin a natural, subtle flush.

SHADE EYELIDS

A soft, brown with a hint of pink enhances eyes natural contours without showing up as shadow. Make sure there are no hard edges while creasing.

ENHANCE LASHES

Defined lashes are essential. Apply two coats to the top lashes. For a boost, use a flat eyeliner brush to grab a bit of mascara from the wand and apply to just the roots of the bottom lashes.

DOT ON EYE PENCIL

Lightly dot a soft gray or brown pencil between the top lashes. This brings eyelashes and your eyelid into one. Day wear should stop even at the edge of your eye.

SUBTLY AMP UP LIPS

Pick a shade that matches your lips exactly and press the color into lips with fingertip. Concentrate it in the center and blend out.

Night Look

Bridal Makeup

LET YOUR EYES DO THE TALKING

Dramatic eyes are an absolute must when it comes to the quintessential Indian bridal makeup. Go bold or go glitter, add fake lashes and layers of mascara, let your eyes be enhanced and make a statement.

BOLD MATTE LIPS

Bridal makeup tips may vary, opinions and choices may differ but the one thing that remains common is – bold lips! Use a bright shade of red or pink to give yourself the perfect pout and stand out against your red bridal lehenga.

CONTOUR ALLURE

Use bronzer to look chiseled and sharp in the photographs. Contouring will accentuate the your features such as the cheek bones and nose but make sure that you do not overdo it.

THE BLUSHING BRIDE

Keep your blush very natural, a soft pink or even a neutral shade for a slight colour. You can add a highlighter to the cheekbones, but steer clear from using a very bright blush colour.

Career Options

PRODUCT DEVELOPMENT

INDEPENDENT ARTIST

BEAUTY WRITER

RUNWAY

THEATRE

PRINT

FILM AND TELEVISION

EDUCATION

COSTUME MAKEUP

RED CARPET AND CELEBRITY

BRIDAL

BRAND REPRESENTATIVE OR RETAIL

SPA/MEDICAL